THE
ECHIDNA

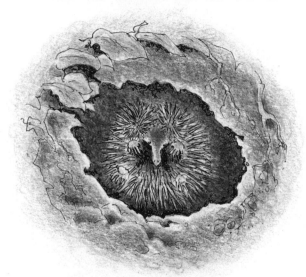

BY PAULINE REILLY

ILLUSTRATED BY WILL ROLLAND

KANGAROO PRESS

We acknowledge with thanks the information
and assistance given by Dr M.L. Augee, Dr Mervyn Griffiths,
Dr Peggy Rismiller and Mr Mike McKelvey.

Reprinted in 1992 and 1996
First published in 1990 by Kangaroo Press Pty Ltd
3 Whitehall Road Kenthurst NSW 2156 Australia
PO Box 6125 Dural Delivery Centre NSW 2158
Printed in Singapore by Kyodo Printing Co (S'pore) Pte Ltd

ISBN 0 86417 285 0

Echidna lived in the forest.

In the autumn, foresters light little fires to burn the leaves and twigs and bark that litter the forest floor.
This is to save the forest from big fires.

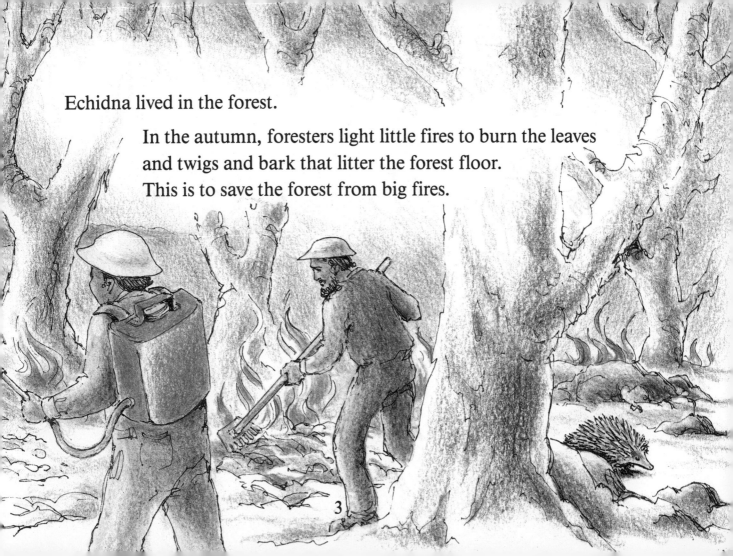

When one of these little fires came towards Echidna,
she dug herself under the ground.
But she did not dig quite deeply enough.
Some of the spines on her back were burnt
and their stumps formed a small round patch.

4

Next day,
Echidna shuffled through the smoking remains of the fire.
As she foraged, she found and ate ants and termites
and the grubs of other insects and sometimes earthworms.

She probed into ant nests and smelt and heard
the ants moving inside.

Her long tongue flicked in and out, up and down,
backwards and forwards and trapped the ants.
They were drawn into the back of her mouth
where they were crushed and swallowed.

In the coldest part of winter, Echidna dug a short burrow
under the root of a tree. She slept.
Her body grew stiff and cold until it was
not much warmer than the air in the burrow.
She did not suffer because she was deeply asleep.

When days grew warmer and spring approached,
Echidna awoke and began to eat again.
She dug a hole in a termite mound and feasted
on the fat white termites and their fat white grub babies.

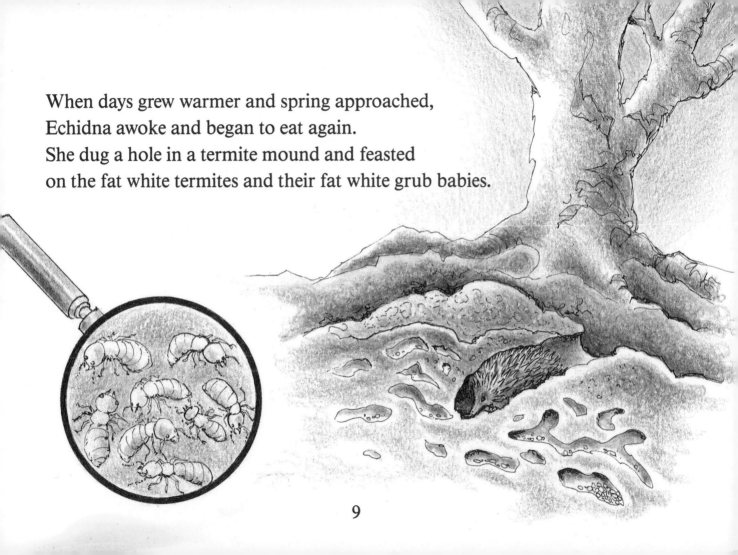

Two male echidnas intent on mating, joined her in foraging.
When they rested, Echidna and the two males huddled together.

10

When Echidna was ready to mate, she anchored her front feet
firmly in the ground. The two males began to dig a trench
round her until one male chased the other away and continued digging.

Sometimes he prodded her tail with his nose
    or lifted it up with his back feet
        or stroked her back spines with his front feet.
When he had dug a deep enough ditch under her tail, they mated.

Echidna dug a burrow under a heap of leaves, then went out to feed.

For three weeks an egg grew inside Echidna.

Then, returning to the burrow and rolling her body into a ball,

she laid the egg into her pouch.

The egg was soft and creamy-coloured and about the size of a small grape.

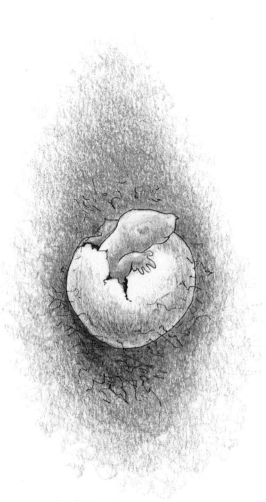

Ten days later, a baby echidna
cut its way out of the egg using the egg tooth
on the end of its snout.

The baby echidna climbed to one of the two
milk patches inside the pouch.
It sucked up its mother's milk.

Sometimes when Echidna went foraging,
she carried her baby in her pouch.
But when it was seven weeks old,
its spines began to grow.
Then she left it sheltered and safe
in the nursery burrow.

She often travelled more than two kilometres
when foraging. But wherever she went,
she always knew the way back and returned to suckle her baby.

The baby slept most of the time, lying in loose fine dirt.

Echidna woke her sleeping baby by nudging it
with her snout. Then she pushed the baby under her body
with her front feet. The baby rolled onto its back,
clung to her belly hair and thrust its head
into her pouch to drink.

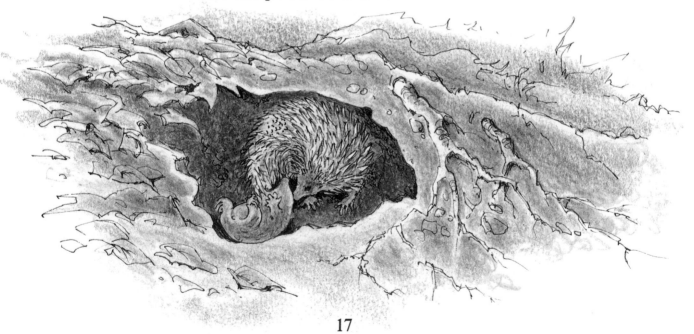

Sometimes she met other echidnas
but they did not fight.
Like all echidnas, she did not own a territory.

When the weather was fine and warm,
she foraged at night as well as in the daytime.

When the weather was hot,
she sheltered below the ground because she could not pant
or sweat to lose heat.

Sometimes she foraged in the rain

or sheltered under a tussock

or in the burrow of another animal

or anywhere dry.

21

One day, she rested inside a hollow log.
A gardener collecting a few pieces of wood
to decorate her garden, lifted the log into the boot of her car
and drove away home.

Echidna crawled out of the log.

Wanting to escape, she scratched up the carpet
with her powerful claws,

ripped open a bag of groceries,

dug furiously into some flour,

sent oats flying everywhere

and split open a bag of fruit.

When the gardener opened the boot, she gasped,
then roared with laughter.

The gardener drove back to the forest.
Echidna rolled herself into a ball to protect herself.
The gardener replaced the hollow log,
put Echidna down beside it and drove away again.

But instead of entering the log,
Echidna dug straight down into the ground under some leaves.

Along came a hungry goanna.
It nosed the moving leaves and then bit into them.
Echidna's spines stuck into its tongue and it ran away.

One sunny day, Echidna came to a stream.
She swam across it in the same way that she walked,
her snout breaking the surface like a snorkel.

She scrambled up the bank on the other side,
using her snout like a fifth leg.

Then she preened between her spines
with the long grooming claws on her back feet.
This helped to rid her of mites and fleas
and especially ticks which **would** crawl into her ear holes.

Early in the autumn when Echidna's baby was six months old,
it had grown big and strong.

It now followed its mother when she went out to feed.
It soon learnt to feed itself.

Soon Echidna's milk and her protection were no longer needed and the young echidna left to live on its own.

In a few years, it would become an echidna parent.

Echidna would have more babies sometime but she would not have one every year.

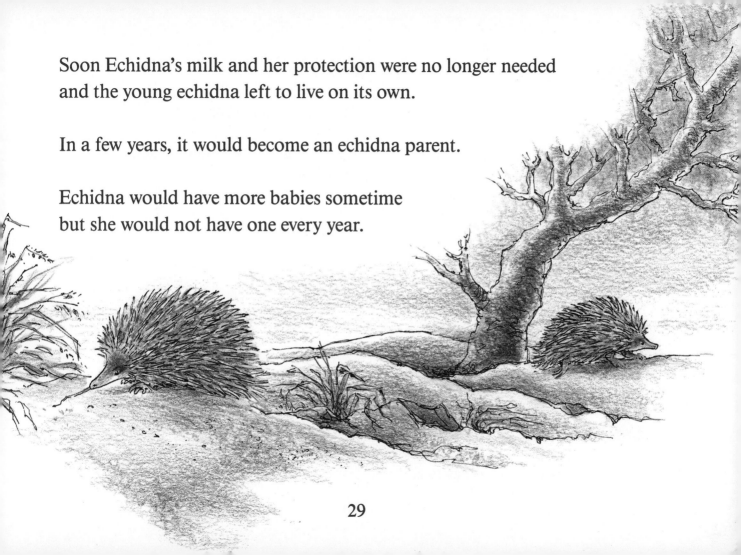

Echidnas used to be called Spiny Anteaters.

They are mammals because they feed their young on milk.

They belong to a special order of mammals called Monotremes.
They are different from other mammals
because they lay eggs and the young do not get their
milk through a teat.

The scientific name of our echidna, the Short-beaked
Echidna, is *Tachyglossus aculeatus*.
(Tacky-gloss'us ah-kyule-ee-ate'-us.)
Tachyglossus means quick tongue and *aculeatus* means
provided with prickles.

The echidna is most closely related to the platypus,
which also lays eggs and suckles its young, but it is
not related to porcupines or hedgehogs, both of which are prickly.
Echidnas and platypuses are more closely related to
each other than to any other living mammals.

Short-beaked Echidna

Echidnas are found all over Australia.
They also live in the lowlands of the New Guinea region
but in the highlands there is another echidna,
the Long-beaked Echidna. It is more
than twice as long and twice as heavy as the Short-beaked.
It stands high on its legs, has a very long and
slightly curved snout and feeds mostly on earthworms.

Long-beaked Echidna

31

Young Short-beaked Echidnas have a hollow spur
on each ankle. The male keeps its spur
but the female sheds it later in life.
The spur does not have venom in it
like the spur carried by the male platypus.

In the wild, echidnas may live for at least 20 years.
One in captivity lived for 49 years.

Dingoes and cats and goannas eat young echidnas
still in their burrows but echidnas are most
in danger when they shuffle slowly across a road.
Then they are killed by cars and trucks.